Henry Van Dyke

Thy Sea is Great - Our Boats are Small

Outlook

Henry Van Dyke

Thy Sea is Great - Our Boats are Small

1. Auflage | ISBN: 978-3-73262-302-0

Erscheinungsort: Frankfurt am Main, Deutschland

Erscheinungsjahr: 2018

Outlook Verlag GmbH, Frankfurt.

Thy Sea is Great
Our Boats are Small

AND

Other Hymns
of To-Day

By

HENRY VAN DYKE

New York   *Chicago*

Fleming H. Revell Company

London and EdinburghCopyright, 1922, by FLEMING
H. REVELL COMPANY

Printed in United States of America

New York: 158 Fifth Avenue
Chicago: 17 North Wabash Ave.
London: 21 Paternoster Square
Edinburgh: 75 Princes Street

FOREWORD

These verses are simple expressions of common Christian feelings and desires in this present time,—hymns of today that may be sung together by people who know the thought of the age, and are not afraid that any truth of science will destroy religion, or any revolution on earth overthrow the kingdom of heaven. Therefore these are hymns of trust and joy and hope.

In the writing, each of them has followed a familiar air, heard in the mind; and the names of these tunes are given. But if some one with the gift of melody should compose new and better music for the hymns, the author would be glad and grateful. As they stand, they are at the service of all who ask and receive the permission of the publishers to use them.

HENRY VAN DYKE.

Avalon

March 30, 1922

I
VOYAGERS

"The sea is his, and he made it."—Ps. XCV:5.

O Maker of the Mighty Deep
    Whereon our vessels fare,
Above our life's adventure keep
    Thy faithful watch and care.
In Thee we trust, whate'er befall;
Thy sea is great, our boats are small.

We know not where the secret tides
    Will help us or delay,
Nor where the lurking tempest hides,
    Nor where the fogs are gray.
We trust in Thee, whate'er befall;
Thy sea is great, our boats are small.

When outward bound we boldly sail
    And leave the friendly shore,
Let not our heart of courage fail
    Until the voyage is o'er.
We trust in Thee, whate'er befall;
Thy sea is great, our boats are small.

When homeward bound we gladly turn,
    O bring us safely there,
Where harbor-lights of friendship burn

And peace is in the air.

We trust in Thee, whate'er befall;

Thy sea is great, our boats are small.

Beyond the circle of the sea,

 When voyaging is past,

We seek our final port in Thee;

 O bring us home at last.

In Thee we trust, whate'er befall;

Thy sea is great, our boats are small.

8.6.8.6.4.4.4.4

Meiringen.

II
THE BURNING BUSH

"I will now turn aside and see this great sight."—Exod. III:3.

Thy wisdom and Thy might appear,
Eternal God, through every year;
From day to day, from hour to hour,
Thy works reveal self-ordered power.

We worship Thee whose will hath laid
Thy sovereign rule on all things made;
The faithful stars, the fruitful earth,
Obey Thy laws that gave them birth.

Yet Thou canst make a marvel shine
Amid these mighty laws of Thine.
As when Thy servant Moses came
And saw the bush with Thee aflame.

We turn aside and tread the ways
That lead through wonder up to praise;
Wherever Thou by man art found
The homely earth is holy ground.

If Thou hast formed us out of dust
Through ages long,—in Thee we trust;
O grant us in our souls to see
The living flame that comes from Thee.

L. M. *Canonbury.*

III
CHILDREN IN THE MARKET-PLACE

"They are like children in the market-place."—L<small>UKE</small> VII:32.

Like children in the market-place
  Who weary of their play,
We turn from folly's idle race
  And come to Thee today.
O Jesus, teller of the tale
  That never will grow old,
Thy words of living truth prevail
  Our listening hearts to hold.
Tell us of Father-love that speaks
  Peace to the wandering child;
Of valiant Shepherd-love that seeks
  The lost sheep in the wild;
Of deep Redeemer-love that knows
  What sins we need forgiven,
And on the Magdalen bestows
  The purest joy of Heaven.
Tell us of faith that's like a sword,
  And hope that's like a star;
How great the patient soul's reward,
  How blest the loyal are.
Tell us of courage like a wall

No storm can batter down;
Tell us of men who venture all
    For Thee, and win a crown.
Tell us that life is not a game,
    But real and brave and true;
A journey with a glorious aim,
    A quest to carry through.
Tell us that though our wills are weak
    And though we children be,
The everlasting good we seek
    We can attain through Thee.

C. M. D.
St. Leonard.

IV
JESUS RETURN

"I will not leave you comfortless: I will come to you."—St. John XIV:18.

Return, dear Lord, to those who look

    With eager eyes that yearn

For Thee among the garden flowers;

After the dark and lonely hours,

    As morning light return.

Return to those who wander far,

    With lamps that dimly burn,

Along the troubled road of thought,

Where doubt and conflict come unsought,—

    With inward joy return.

Return to those on whom the yoke

    Of life is hard and stern;

Renew the hope within their breast,

Draw them to Thee and give them rest;

    O Friend of Man, return.

Return to this war-weary world,

    And help us all to learn

Thy secret of victorious life,

The love that triumphs over strife,—

    O prince of Peace, return.

Jesus, we ask not now that day

When all men shall discern Thy
coming with the angelic host;
Today, to all who need Thee most,
In silent ways, return!

8.6.8.8.6

Elton.

V
ONE IN CHRIST

"Other sheep I have, which are not of this fold."—St. John X:16.

No form of human framing,
  No bond of outward might,
Can bind Thy Church together, Lord,
  And all her flocks unite;
But, Jesus, Thou hast told us
  How unity must be:
Thou art with God the Father one,
  And we are one in Thee.

The mind that is in Jesus
  Will guide us into truth,
The humble, open, joyful mind
  Of ever-learning youth;
The heart that is in Jesus
  Will lead us out of strife,
The giving and forgiving heart
  That follows love in life.

Wherever men adore Thee,
  Our souls with them would kneel;
Wherever men implore Thy help,
  Their trouble we would feel;
And where men do Thy service,

Though knowing not Thy sign,
Our hand is with them in good work,
   For they are also Thine.
Forgive us, Lord, the folly
   That quarrels with Thy friends,
And draw us nearer to Thy heart
   Where every discord ends;
Thou art the crown of manhood,
   And Thou of God the Son;
O Master of our many lives,
   In Thee our life is one.

7.6.8.6.D.
Alford.

VI
FOUNDATIONS

"Those things which cannot be shaken"—H<small>EB</small>. XII:28.

Now again the world is shaken,

   Tempests break on sea and shore;

Earth with ruin overtaken,

   Trembles while the storm-winds roar.

     He abideth who confideth,

   God is God forevermore.

Thrones are falling, heathen raging,

   Peoples dreaming as of yore

Vain imaginations, waging

   Man with man, unmeaning war.

     He abideth who confideth,

   Christ is King forevermore.

Human wisdom in confusion,

   Casts away the forms it wore;

Ancient error, new illusion,

   Lose the phantom fruit they bore,

     He abideth who confideth,

   Truth is truth forevermore.

Right eternal, Love immortal,

   Built the House where we adore;

Mercy is its golden portal,

Virtue its unshaken floor.

    He abideth who confideth,

    God is God forevermore.

8.7.8.7.4.4.7.

Regent Square.

VII
VICTORIA

"Be of good cheer, I have overcome the world."—St. John XVI:33.

Thy victory is in the heart,

  Thy kingdom is within;

When outward pride and pomp depart,

  Thy glory doth begin.

Thine army, ever in the field,

  Is led by love and light;

Thy followers fall but never yield,

  Triumphant in the right.

O King most meek and wonderful,

  Grant us among Thy host,

To follow Thee, to fight for Thee,

  Knights of the Holy Ghost.

C. M.

St. Anne.

THREE EARLIER HYMNS

Hymn of Joy

Peace Hymn of the Republic

—From "Poems of Henry van Dyke"

 Copyright 1911-1920 by

 Charles Scribner's Sons.

HYMN OF LABOR

Jesus, Thou divine Companion,

 By Thy lowly human birth

Thou hast come to join the workers,

 Burden-bearers of the earth.

Thou, the Carpenter of Naz'reth,

 Toiling for Thy daily food,

By Thy patience and Thy courage,

 Thou hast taught us toil is good.

They who tread the path of labor

 Follow where Thy feet have trod;

They who work without complaining

 Do the holy will of God.

Thou, the peace that passeth knowledge,

 Dwellest in the daily strife;

Thou, the Bread of heaven, art broken

 In the sacrament of life.

Every task, however simple,

 Sets the soul that does it free;

Every deed of love and kindness

 Done to man is done to Thee.

Jesus, Thou divine Companion,

 Help us all to work our best;

Bless us in our daily labor,

    Lead us to our Sabbath rest.

8.7.8.7.D

Beecher.

HYMN OF JOY

Joyful, joyful, we adore Thee,
  God of glory, Lord of love;
Hearts unfold like flowers before Thee,
  Praising Thee their sun above.
Melt the clouds of sin and sadness;
  Drive the dark of doubt away;
Giver of immortal gladness,
  Fill us with the light of day!
All Thy works with joy surround Thee,
  Earth and heaven reflect Thy rays,
Stars and angels sing around Thee,
  Centre of unbroken praise:
Field and forest, vale and mountain,
  Blooming meadow, billowing sea,
Chanting bird and flowing fountain,
  Call us to rejoice in Thee.
Thou art giving and forgiving,
  Ever blessing, ever blest,
Well-spring of the joy of living,
  Ocean-depth of happy rest.
Thou our Father, Christ our Brother,—
  All who live in love are Thine:

Teach us how to love each other,

    Lift us to the Joy Divine.

Mortals join the mighty chorus,

    Which the morning stars began;

Father-love is reigning o'er us,

    Brother-love binds man to man.

Ever singing march we onward,

    Victors in the midst of strife;

Joyful music lifts us sunward

    In the triumph song of life.

8.7.8.7.D

Music from Beethoven's Ninth Symphony.

PEACE HYMN OF THE REPUBLIC

O Lord, our God, Thy mighty hand
    Hath made our country free;
From all her broad and happy land
    May praise arise to Thee.
Fulfil the promise of her youth,
    Her liberty defend;
By law and order, love and truth,
    America befriend!

The strength of every state increase
    In Union's golden chain;
Her thousand cities fill with peace,
    Her million fields with grain.
The virtues of her mingled blood
    In one new people blend;
By unity and brotherhood
    America befriend!

O suffer not her feet to stray;
    But guide her untaught might,
That she may walk in peaceful day,
    And lead the world in light.
Bring down the proud, lift up the poor,
    Unequal ways amend;

By justice, nation-wide and sure,
    America befriend!
Through all the waiting land proclaim
    Thy gospel of good-will;
And may the music of Thy name
    In every bosom thrill.
O'er hill and vale, from sea to sea,
    Thy holy reign extend;
By faith and hope and charity,
    America befriend!

C.M.D.

Materna.